The Boy Who Ate America

To my family, who believe in dreams—NJ

For my family and the children I don't have yet—CN

Text © 2007 Nathan Smith Jones

Illustrations © 2007 Casey Nelson

Design by Meridith Ethington

Visit us at ShadowMountain.com

Library of Congress Cataloging-in-Publication Data
[CIP on file]
ISBN: 978-1-59038-814-3

Printed in China
Phoenix Color

10   9   8   7   6   5   4   3   2   1

The Boy WHo Ate America

BY NATHAN SMITH JONES
ILLUSTRATED BY CASEY NELSON

SHADOW
MOUNTAIN

There once was a boy—sounds crazy but true—who ate the whole country, and Hawaii, too!

He said to his mother, "I'm hungry," one day.
"You ate lunch at two!" she said with dismay

"But I'm so very hungry," he started to whine.
But his mom wasn't dumb. She knew he'd be fine.

She asked with a smirk, "Then what should you do?"
So off to the kitchen he went for more food.

He opened the fridge and had him some pie, then wolfed down a sandwich and left-over Thai.

"I'm still so hungry!" he spoke to himself, as he grabbed some more cookies from the very top shelf.

COOKI

And a big, squeaky ROAR from his tummy in need, gave proof to the boy that his stomach agreed.

But then the boy's eyes turned
bright as his luck
When he heard the jing-ling
of an ice cream truck.

His mouth filled with hope
and his mind filled with song
at the thought that these
cravings would finally
be gone!

But after he downed every Chocolate Crunch Treat, he took a **HUGE** bite of the ice cream truck's seat!

The owners of cars on the street looked with fright
as their cars all fell victim to the boy's appetite.

He ate them all up and gobbled them down,
and soon he was eating the whole stinkin' TOWN!

Windows and buildings and schools and malls—
he even ate broccoli with pink bathroom stalls!

His mouth **stretched** as far and as wide as it needed
then shrank back to normal right after he feeded.

He ate up the stores and the banks a day later.
He ate all his teachers and even the mayor!

Then all of the people in his stomach complained that being down in his insides was really a pain!

"Being rained on by soda and billboards and gum and napping with thousands down here isn't fun!"

"I'm sorry," he said, "I don't mean any harm," while the boy took a bite from the side of a barn.

"Why don't I get **BIGGER?**" he wondered aloud, as all that he ate showered down on the crowd.

The goat and the chickens and the old farmer's bull swallowed up by the boy who still wasn't full.

No time to do house chores or even to play,
the boy now ate **more** than a city a day!

He snacked on La Jolla 'cause Blythe made him thinner,
had Oakland for lunch, Sacramento for dinner!

And then before thinking of how it would taste, he then went from cities to chomping down states!

Nevada on Tuesday with gold-dollar jelly. Arizona, New Mexico snug in his belly.

Now Texas took two days 'cause it was GIGANTIC! Then 'Bama and Georgia to reach the Atlantic.

He sprinkled Virginia all over the coast, then swallowed New York like a cinnamon toast.

He had Boston with beans
and Houston with ham,
Salt Lake City with Jell-O
and L.A. with Spam.

He noshed on Seattle and
chewed on Duluth
(after getting the Space
Needle out of his tooth).

He munched on the Redwoods
like chips and some dip,
then washed it all down with the
'ol Mississip.

The mid-state of Kansas was all that was left,
with all of its refugees feeling bereft.

The governor begged for the young man to stop,
and he **puffed** out his chest all angry and hot.

"Young man now, young man now, you hear me, I pray!
Our fair state will NOT be your next grand buffet!"

"I'm sorry! I'm sorry! I wish that I could!"
And soon it was water where Kansas once stood.

In a raft with his mom and nothing to do,
he still felt so hungry, and GUILTY now, too!

Water and water was all he could see.
He still wasn't full. What else could there be?

"Son, maybe your body's not hungry a bit,"
she said, wiping part of Detroit from his lip.

"See, people feel empty a lot these days
and they try to fill it up in all sorts of ways.

"Some fill it with food or anger or wine,
some fill it with work or excuses or lying.

"Some fill it with money or clothing or toys,
some fill it with drama or tension or noise.

"But the emptiness never gets filled with that stuff.
They fill and they fill, but it's never enough.

"We're all hungry, son," she tried to imbue.
"Your body needs food, but your soul needs
some too!"

So she gave him God's words, and with a
lovingly tone, said, "Man shall not live
by just bread alone."

Then right after feeling the
strangest sensation,
from out of his foot popped
the **entire** nation!

There was Florida, Montana, Vermont, and Nebraska, and then came Wisconsin, New York, and Alaska!

But now the whole country was all **such a mess!**
Rocky Mountains in Pittsburgh! Times Square was out West!

But finally everyone offered to help
to clean off Mount Rushmore all covered with kelp.

They moved the Grand Canyon back where it should be;
put all the lighthouses of Maine by the sea,

And when every city
was back in its place,
and everyone happy,
gave thanks, and said grace,

Then the boy sat down by his bedroom door,
and he read, and he hungered and thirsted no more.